HOCUS AND POCUS

and the Spell for Home

HOCUS AND POCUS

and the Spell for Home

A. R. Capetta

illustrated by Charlene Chua

CANDLEWICK PRESS

Text copyright © 2024 by A. R. Capetta
Illustrations copyright © 2024 by Charlene Chua

First edition 2024

Library of Congress Catalog Card Number 2023944125
ISBN 978-1-5362-2492-4 (hardcover)
ISBN 978-1-5362-3672-9 (paperback)

24 25 26 27 28 29 APS 10 9 8 7 6 5 4 3 2 1

Printed in Humen, Dongguan, China

This book was typeset in ITC Mendoza.
The illustrations were created digitally.

Candlewick Press
99 Dover Street
Somerville, Massachusetts 02144

www.candlewick.com

For Maverick, Rey, and Poe
ARC

For Ladybird Animal Sanctuary—
thank you for your work.
CC

Chapter One

Slightly Magical Puppies

Hocus and Pocus were born in late October, when even the wind was full of mischief.

A witch found their entire litter wandering outside as the last of the leaves fell. She could tell they were too small to stay out in the cold. They needed homes with soft laps and plenty of treats. She could also tell the pups were slightly magical. They needed witches, wizards, and warlocks who would take care of them.

This witch wanted to help. She took the litter to the Shelter for Slightly Magical Pets.

The shelter held a slew of bewitching kittens, dozens of enchanted fish, three charmed chinchillas, and a sad tortoise whose shell changed colors when it rained.

"It's good to have you here," the human who owned the shelter told them. "You probably won't stay long, though. People love puppies. Magical humans are always looking for magical puppies. You are all slightly magical and more than slightly adorable."

Hocus, who had been born first, was the biggest of the litter. Her coat was partly white and partly the color of sweet, salty caramel. The thing that made her slightly magical was this: she could stare deep into a person's eyes and see what would happen in exactly two minutes.

Pocus, who had been born last, stayed little. His coat was white with spots like chocolate sprinkles, and his head was the

color of a perfect cup of hot cocoa. The thing that made him slightly magical was this: he could snuggle up to you and any bad feeling you had would float away. First Pocus turned it into a brightly colored bubble. Then he ate the bubble with a *snap* of his jaws.

Double, Toil, and Trouble each had enchanted ears that could pick up the sound of a spell being cast miles away. Whenever they saw a witch, wizard, or warlock, they ran up and flipped over for a belly rub. All three were adopted within days.

Hocus and Pocus wanted a home, too. But they didn't want to go to *different* homes the way Double, Toil, and Trouble had. They wanted a home *together*.

"What do we do?" Pocus asked, gnawing the shark slipper he'd borrowed from the shelter owner. "Someone will take you first, I know it. I'll never see you again!"

"Unacceptable," Hocus grumbled. "We'll use our magic to stop it."

"What if that's not enough?" Pocus asked.

"Then we'll use our mischief, too."

Chapter Two

Too Much Mischief?

When a warlock and witch couple came in the next day and asked to look at puppies, Hocus stared deep into their eyes.

"Oh no," she said. "In exactly two minutes, they'll ask to adopt one of us! *Only one!*" Hocus knew it would be her, but she didn't want to make Pocus even more nervous, so she didn't add that detail.

"No!" Pocus cried, already nervous enough. "We have to stop it!"

Pocus leaped into the witch's arms.

Hocus squatted low.

Hocus had what the shelter owner called "an accident"—but this was an "on purpose."

The warlock danced around, shouting, "It's getting on my robes!" Pocus turned all their bad feelings into bubbles and ate them. He didn't want these people to be *too* mad at Hocus.

But they definitely didn't adopt anyone.

Another day, a wizard came in with a small wizard-baby and a wand that looked like an excellent fetch stick. "I'm looking for one perfect pet who will grow up along with my little one."

"Just *one* pet," Hocus said.

"Mischief time!" Pocus shouted.

Hocus climbed the wizard like a tree.

Hocus slurped a hundred kisses on the wizard-baby's face.

Pocus grabbed the wizard's wand while they were distracted and did what he did best: power chew.

He spent the next two days burping sparks.

The shelter human shook their head. "This might be harder than I thought. You've been here for months and nobody's even filled out an application."

Pocus had actually eaten several applications.

"What if no one ever adopts us?" Pocus asked. "What if our mischief is backfiring? Like a wand when you chew on it?"

"Hmmm," Hocus grumbled. "Maybe we have to stop thinking about what we *don't* want . . ."

"We don't want to get split up!" Pocus yelped.

"And spend time trying to get what we *do* want."

"We want treats and a person to give us lots of treats," Pocus helped.

"We want a home. Together. Right?" Hocus had to help her little brother along sometimes. He needed someone to talk him into things. "We'll be extra good when the next magical human comes in, okay?"

"We're *good dogs*," Pocus said, but he didn't sound so sure.

Right at that moment, a witch burst through the door. The same witch who'd

brought them to the shelter in the first place.

Hocus said, "We'll be this witch's puppies in no time."

But the witch had other ideas.

Chapter Three

A Witch Called Jinx

The witch waved around a potion and said, "I'm here to see a very sad tortoise."

Hocus knew she could convince this witch they'd be more fun than a tortoise who only poked his head out once a week. All he did was eat a head of lettuce. Pocus, on the other hand, ate one shoe from every pair he found. Even their snacking was more exciting.

"Are you here to find pets?" Hocus asked, sitting at the witch's feet. "We're *good dogs*."

Of course, Hocus didn't expect the witch to understand exactly what she was saying. She'd never met a human who could speak puppy.

"Good to meet you again, pups," the witch said as she crouched down in front of them. "My name is Abigail Verona Esme Jinx. The pronouns she and her are good for me. And everyone just calls me Jinx."

"What a good name," Pocus said.

"What a good smell!" Hocus cried. She remembered it from their first meeting. Jinx smelled like magic, her very own sort. Like herbs and candles and forests.

"Yes," Pocus agreed. "A truly nice-smelling witch. She really should adopt us."

"You know, I would have bet the barn that you two would have homes by now. I would take you myself . . . But I already have three apprentices to keep track of. Besides, my house is too messy for pets. It's a delightful mess, though. Cauldrons everywhere. But when I come here, I get to visit *all* the pets, and I bring some magic in return."

She handed potions over to the shelter owner—more and more potions.

"Here's everything you asked for," she said. "Spells for shedding, spells for fussy stomachs, spells to the keep the fish from eating the aquarium rocks. And one spell for home."

"What's a spell for home?" Pocus asked. "Can you eat it?"

The puppies followed Jinx like two fuzzy shadows. She took the potion over to the tortoise—who poked his head out right away, even though there was no lettuce in sight.

Jinx really *was* magic.

"If a pet has been here for a long time, or seems sad to not have found a family yet, I can help." Jinx took out a clipper.

She trimmed a single nail from the tortoise's ancient toe. "There are three ingredients in the spell for home. The first is water from happy tears. The second is a pinch of dirt from a special place. And the last comes from the pet-to-be. A bit of fur, a feather or two. For our tortoise friend, a toenail will work."

Hocus watched with wide, glowing eyes as Jinx dropped the toenail into the vial and swirled it around.

"This will help nudge the right person in the right direction." Jinx sat down on the floor. No humans ever sat on the floor with Hocus and Pocus. "Now we wait."

Ten minutes later, a teenage warlock walked in the door, looking a little confused.

"I'm not sure why I'm here," the warlock said. "I . . ."

"Need a tortoise?" Jinx asked, leaping up. "Of course you do!"

"But I'm a weather warlock. I'm always making it snow in the middle of summer. A lot of pets don't like that."

"Can you make it rain, by any chance?" Jinx asked.

"Whoa," the warlock said.

As the shelter grew sunny again, Hocus and Pocus put their noses close to the potion and watched it change—from bright yellow to dark, dark blue. "That's how you know you've found the right person," Jinx said. "It turns the color of comfort."

The weather warlock tucked the tortoise under one arm and left.

"And that, pups, is the spell for home," Jinx said.

Chapter Four

A Dark and Bumpy Ride

Hocus was impressed. And she had an idea.

She patted her paw on Jinx's foot. She pointed her nose directly at the potion.

"Hmmm," Jinx said. "You want a spell for home, too?"

"They could use it," the shelter owner said. "They're sweet dogs, but they cause so much mischief it's scaring everyone off."

Jinx looked at them with a squint. "I think I have enough for two more spells. I'll bring them tomorrow."

"What?" Pocus yelped. "Now she's going to make us separate potions, and we'll get split up for sure!"

"Or," Hocus huffed, "we follow her home and make sure a hair from each of us gets into *one* potion."

While Jinx talked to the shelter owner, Hocus slunk into the witch's bag.

"Come on!" she whispered to Pocus. "Get in."

This was the wildest idea Hocus had ever had.

Pocus did *not* think it was going to work.

But he had to help his big sister sometimes. She was filled with ideas and bravery, but she needed a friend at her side. So with a nervous little shiver, he climbed into the bag.

"I do not like this," Hocus grumbled as they started to move. "I do not like this at all."

"It was your plan to go home with Jinx," Pocus reminded his sister.

"I didn't know she was going to *fly*."

Jinx's house was a highly magical place. The outside was bright purple.

The inside was covered in crystals and cauldrons and cobwebs.

Jinx carried her bag into the kitchen and set it down. As soon as she was gone, Hocus and Pocus snuck out and sniffed around. Hocus ate a cobweb. Just to try it.

"We have to find where Jinx makes her potions and . . . Pocus?"

Pocus's head popped up from a small cauldron. "Hocus! I like it here! Do we have to go back to the Shelter for Slightly Magical Pets? This house is so big, I bet we could stay and not bother Jinx at all."

"I think she would notice two puppies living right under her nose. Even if human

noses aren't good at smelling," Hocus said.

Just then, the puppies heard footsteps—but they couldn't belong to Jinx. They were coming from the opposite direction.

Pocus spun in tiny circles. "Who's coming? A stranger? Should we defend the house? For Jinx?"

Hocus got ready to bark her loudest BARK.

Pocus put out one! terrifying! fang!

Chapter Five

What Are Apprentices?

As it turned out, the footsteps belonged to a kid. Hocus rushed up to say hello. Pocus kept the fang out, just in case.

"Where did you two come from?" the kid asked, petting Hocus. She didn't let just anyone rub her belly, but she liked this human right away. "My name's Archer, I'm a witch, and my pronouns are he and him. I'm one of Jinx's apprentices."

"I forgot about the apprentices," Hocus said. "Jinx told us she has three."

"Right," Pocus said. "Hocus, what are apprentices?"

"Magic students."

"Does that mean there are two more kids?"

Hocus scented the air. Her ears perked. Her tail whapped. "I smell one of them right now!" She started to run.

"What about the potion?" Pocus asked. "Don't we have to find the potion?"

Hocus was off to find something just as important. *Friends.*

She ran until she found a garden at the center of the house, and a second kid swinging an enchanted sword.

"Hey!" Hocus shouted. Then she sneezed.

"Hey, little one," the second kid said, before seeing Pocus, who was shaking under a sparkly rosebush. "Sorry—little two. My name is Ofelia and I'm a wizard. My pronouns are she and her. Who are you?"

"Don't tell her!" Pocus said.

"It doesn't matter if I do," Hocus reminded Pocus, "because she can't understand what I'm saying." Plus, Hocus liked this human. She let Ofelia rub her belly, too.

While Ofelia was scritching and scratching, she noticed the tag. "Lovely to meet you, Hocus."

"Now we're really in trouble," Pocus said. "What if she tells the shelter owner?"

"I won't care," Hocus said. "This belly rub is worth it."

"I could pet you all day, but it's practice time," Ofelia said. "Wizards like me spend years on magical sword skills. Today I'm working on a move that makes the other person sneeze."

"That's fine because we are busy," Pocus said. He trotted back toward the house.

Hocus's nose stretched out. She was trying to sniff out the third apprentice, but Ofelia was a little too good at sword practice. Hocus! kept! sneezing!

"I can barely smell anyone else . . . just a faint little hint . . ."

"Hocus!" Pocus shouted. "What about the potion?"

"I need to meet one more friend," Hocus whined. "Just one?"

"We need to find the potion! Not because I'm afraid of meeting new people but because it's very important!" They both knew the truth, though. Pocus got nervous about new people. And animals. And places. And smells. And tastes. And blankets. And chew toys. And . . .

By the time he got to the end of the list, Hocus had taken off.

Pocus sped after her.

"I'm looking for the potion room!" he shouted.

"I'm sniffing out the third apprentice!" she cried.

They skittered around, nosing open door after door. Finally, Pocus smelled something interesting. But this door was shut tight. He put out a paw and scratch-scratch-scratched.

The door swung open from the inside.

It wasn't the potion room. It was a closet, with lots of coats and a third kid, hanging upside down like a bat. The interesting smell probably came from the homemade leather bat wings.

"Oh!" Pocus said. "I'm sorry to interrupt your upside-down time."

"I could tell from the sound of your claws that you must be a dog," the kid said. "I love dogs. I'm Tam the warlock. My pronouns are they and them."

"Hi, Tam!" Pocus yipped.

"What's your name?" Tam asked.

"Pocus," he said, but of course to Tam, it sounded like *Yip!*

"I'm a plant and animal warlock, but I can't speak puppy yet," Tam said with an upside-down frown. "Jinx knows a little bit. I've been working on frog all year and I can only say *Thanks for the flies.*"

Of course, to Pocus, this sounded like *Rrriiiiibit.*

"Very froggish," Pocus said. To make sure Tam didn't feel sad about not speaking puppy, he nuzzled right up to them, and Tam's worries turned into a bright-orange bubble.

"Is that your magic?" Tam asked. "Have you met Jinx yet? This is her house. I really think she would like you."

Pocus wanted to believe that. But if Jinx really liked them, wouldn't she have brought them home? On purpose?

Hocus ran over. "Pocus, I found the potion room."

"I'm not ready to leave," he said. "I found a friend! Their name is Tam and they are the nicest warlock and we snuggled . . ."

Hocus was staring deep, deep, deep into Tam's eyes. Her magic showed her what would happen next.

"The littlest warlock is going to get Jinx," Hocus said.

"Jinx will take us back to the shelter," Pocus added. "Which means we only have two minutes to find the spell and make sure it works!"

Hocus and Pocus dashed toward the potion room.

Chapter Six

Sneakery

The potion room was the best room Hocus
and Pocus had seen yet.

To begin with, it had a tree growing
in the middle of it. A huge black oak tree
with spiky leaves. It didn't look like a tree
someone had brought inside the house.

It looked like the tree was *part* of the house. A spell book sat right in the center of the trunk. There were so many dark red leaves above them, Hocus couldn't tell if the room had a ceiling.

Around the tree was a ring of cauldrons. Inside them, potions bubbled and fizzed.

"This room is filled with spells," Hocus said. "The one we need must be here! But how do we find it?"

"It's yellow," Pocus said. "Bright yellow."

"Time for a little sneakery," Hocus said.

She stuck her nose into the nearest cauldron.

Pocus ran over, carrying one of Jinx's bat-print sneakers.

"Not that kind of sneak! *This* kind of sneak," said Hocus.

"Oh!" Pocus said. "Sneak snoot!"

It was one of Hocus's best moves. Her long snoot could reach into any cup or crevice. Usually, Hocus would lap up whatever she could find. She liked the lemon tea that the shelter owner drank.

"Be careful!" Pocus said. "What if you taste an exploding potion? What if you drink a spell that turns you into a cat?"

Hocus couldn't think of anything worse than being stuck as a cat when you were truly a dog.

Besides being separated from Pocus, of course. She was brave, but a lot of that bravery was Hocus showing her brother that the world wasn't quite as scary as he thought.

Working hard to keep her tongue to herself, Hocus snuck her snoot into every cauldron in the room. She snuck her snoot into a potion that smelled like cupcakes. She snuck her snoot into a potion that smelled like onions. She snuck her snoot into a potion that smelled like dirty socks—delicious.

Then, "Here!" she said. "I found it!"

A potion that smelled like salt and dirt. It was bright yellow, just like the one Jinx had shown them at the shelter. It just needed one final, special ingredient.

Hocus shook and shook, shedding hair into the spell for home. "All right," she said. "Pocus, it's your turn."

He shook and shook. His hair flew everywhere, and some of it landed in the next cauldron over. That one wasn't a spell for home. That was a spell for turning very, very small.

Pocus was already very, very small.

By the time the potion was done with him, he was about the size of an ant.

"Help me, Hocus!" Pocus shouted in a tiny voice.

"How?" Hocus asked. All she could think about was the littlest apprentice running to tell Jinx about the puppies.

The witch would find Hocus being sneaky in her potion room. She would never find Pocus. He was much too tiny. Leaving an ant-size Pocus and going back to the Shelter for Slightly Magical Pets alone was even worse than getting split up when they were normal-size.

"Do some mischief!" Pocus told his sister.

He was right. It was time to take her mischief off the leash.

She looked at the cauldron Pocus had accidentally shed fur into. Hocus couldn't speak human, not the whole language, but she knew a lot of human words. She had even learned the alphabet from a picture book Pocus had eaten. This potion was marked *S*. For *small*!

She found a spell marked with a *B* and poured it all over the floor. "*B* must stand for *big*," she said. "Just stay there and wait to get big again, Pocus."

But Jinx wasn't just any witch, and her spells weren't always labeled in ways that other people—or puppies—could understand.

B didn't stand for *big*.

It stood for *bees*.

Chapter Seven

Bees!

"Why does Jinx have a potion that turns into bees?" Pocus asked in a tiny voice as a swarm of stripes and stingers swirled around the potion room.

Hocus wanted to fix this—but how? "I can eat the bees!"

"Please do not eat bees!" Pocus shouted. "They are much bigger than I am. We need a potion that can turn me Pocus-size again."

Hocus ran around the room in frantic circles. She passed a potion with a big *L* on it. As she made another loop, she thought hard.

If *B* didn't stand for *big*, *L* had to stand for *large*—right?

Hocus nosed the cauldron and tipped the potion out.

But it wasn't just any *large* potion. The only thing it made larger was the last spell you did. Now there were bumblebees growing, and growing, while tiny Pocus stayed tiny. Just as the bees reached puppy size, Jinx came into the room.

"Oh, bats. What happened in here? Tam told me they heard some big buzzing, and now I know why!"

Hocus huffed. That was the trick with her magic. It showed what would happen in two minutes, but not *why* or *how*. If she hadn't spilled the bee potion, maybe Tam wouldn't have fetched Jinx and they wouldn't have gotten caught. But it was too late to undo that.

"These bumblebees are as big as Tam!"
Jinx cried.

Hocus hid behind a cauldron while Pocus tried not to be stepped on. Maybe if nobody found them, they wouldn't get in trouble. Besides, the humans were busy with the bees, which were now the size of ponies, and still growing.

"All right, apprentices," Jinx said. "There's no time to brew a counter-spell. We'll have to deal with this ourselves."

Archer flew up on a broom and tried to chase the bees out the windows. Ofelia waved her magical sword, a bee put out its stinger, and they dueled.

Tam, the littlest warlock, stood in the center of the room and began to dance the way that bees dance when they want to talk to each other. And maybe Tam didn't speak puppy or know much frog, but they were good at bee dancing.

Tam wiggled and spun. Tam bumbled and breezed. The bees stopped to watch. Then they danced a little bit, too, and flew away.

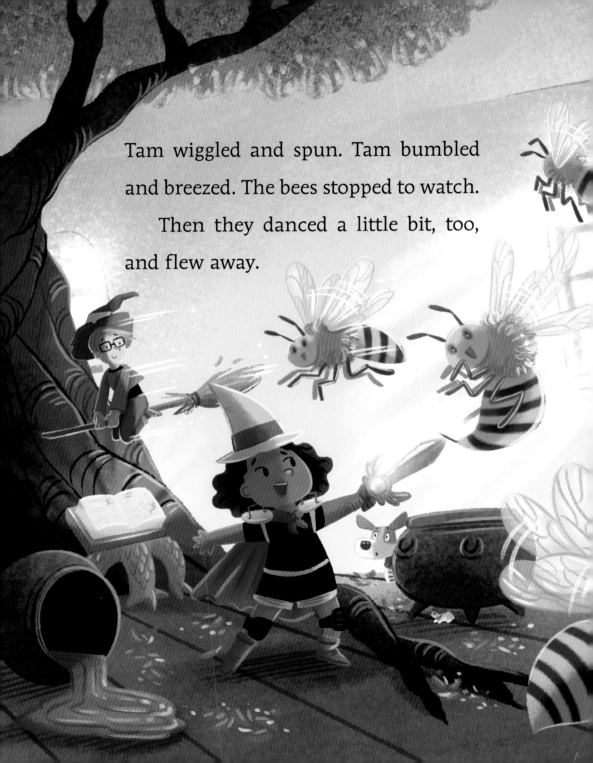

"Why was there a potion that made enormous bees?" Ofelia asked.

"That's what I wanted to know!" Hocus said.

"Well, they were meant to be bee-size bees," Jinx explained. "And they're important to the ecosystem. There aren't enough to go around. So I thought I'd spell a few more to help the flowers along."

"What did you tell the bees?" Archer asked Tam.

"That's what I wanted to know," Pocus added in his tiny voice.

"The best pollen is in the next field over," Tam said. "Nobody lives there. And there are some very nice wildflowers."

"Are you serious?" Hocus asked gruffly. "Even the *gigantic bees* get a home?"

"Did you just hear a dog . . . complaining?" Tam asked.

"There were two dogs in the house today," Ofelia added.

"Dogs?" Jinx asked. "What dogs?"

She looked around the potion room. Pocus was starting to get bigger—he had just reached the size of a teacup.

"Hocus and Pocus. I should have known. This is the most mischief I've ever seen in one place."

Pocus wasn't listening. He had just gotten big enough to see into the cauldron behind Jinx, the one with the spell for home. It had turned from bright, bright yellow to dark, dark blue.

The color of comfort. The color of home.

"Look!" Pocus said.

"Pocus," Hocus said. "It *worked*."

"That means we're supposed to live here with Jinx," Pocus said. "And nap in our own little cauldrons! And eat bat jerky! And play with the apprentices every day!"

Hocus patted her paw on Jinx's foot. She pointed her nose at the spell.

Jinx scooped them up and carried them out of her potion room. She didn't even notice that they belonged with her forever.

Chapter Eight

A Sad Bubble

"We'll find you nice homes," the shelter owner told Hocus and Pocus the next morning. "I promise."

The shelter owner had been surprised that Hocus and Pocus snuck away with Jinx. But not *that* surprised. Maybe they really were too much mischief for anyone to want both of them.

Pocus was back to his regular size now. He never thought he'd be happy to call himself a very small dog, but after trying life as a furry ant, this felt much better.

Hocus had spent all night trying to think of a new plan to keep them together, but she didn't have a single idea—or any bravery—left.

"There's a witch here who wants to see puppies," the shelter owner called out.

Hocus and Pocus didn't want to meet a new witch.

They wanted Jinx.

But the voice they heard sounded very . . . Jinx-ish.

"When I was cleaning up last night, I saw the spell for home," she said. "And how blue it was."

"You did?" Pocus asked.

"It's a lot of work to keep track of three apprentices, but they all swore they would help take care of puppies."

"They did?" Pocus asked.

"And my house needed to be cleaned up and puppy-proofed . . ."

"*It did?*" Pocus asked.

Hocus turned her back on Jinx and walked away. "We're too much mischief," she said. "You'll end up bringing us right back to the Shelter for Slightly Magical Pets."

Hocus didn't want that to be true. But she was too scared to believe that Jinx was their witch. She was afraid of getting her heart broken.

Jinx scooped Hocus up in her arms. "I'm not mad about the bees. In fact, I'm making huge pots of honey for everyone in Inkwell, thanks to you. And I'll love you two just as much, no matter how much mischief you are. Besides, a little mischief is good for a witch."

"Are you sure?" Hocus asked.

Jinx really must have known how to speak a bit of puppy, because she said, "I'm sure."

"You know, I've never seen a dog finish a spell before," she added. "I'm not sure you're slightly magical puppies at all. I think you might be *highly* magical puppies."

"Hmm," Hocus said. "*Highly* magical?"

"At my house, you'll have the chance to use your magic every single day. And learn new magic, too."

"Thank you for giving me a chance, Hocus and Pocus."

Pocus's magic made a purple bubble float up. He ate it with a snap of his jaws.

"That was a sad bubble," Pocus said.

"Why is Jinx sad?" Hocus asked.

"She feels bad that she didn't notice we were supposed to be her puppies right from the start. But now she feels better, and I helped! Also, I forgive her."

"Yes," Hocus said wisely. "She really needed the spell for home."

Exactly Two Minutes Later

Hocus didn't need to look deep, deep, deep into Jinx's eyes. She already knew what would be happening in two minutes.

Jinx would fill out an application.

Pocus would not eat it.

DON'T MISS!

HOCUS AND POCUS

and the Dragon Next Door

Look for the next book in the series, coming in spring 2025!